To my Centennial
Buddies –
Wash those
Hands!
Germs... Yeech...

DRINKING FOUNTAIN JOE

JUSTIN MATOTT
ILLUSTRATIONS · DAVID SCHIEDT

Library of Congress
Cataloging-in-Publication Data
Matott, Justin.
Drinking Fountain Joe/
written by Justin Matott;
illustrated by
David Schiedt - 1st ed. p. cm.

Summary: an odd, slightly
bearded elementary student
discovers the cure to baldness
while trying to eradicate his
school of germs and make a
little spending cash toward
a future fortune.

ISBN 1-889191-12-4
{1. Inventor-Fiction.
2. Science-Fiction}
I. David Schiedt 1954-ill. II.
Title First edition A B C D E
Printed in Hong Kong

For JJ and Ethan
And Mr. Colburn a wonderful
teacher who once looked upon this
"Joe" with kinder eyes than most.
-J. M.
For Gail, Nellie and Tiffany.
-D. S.
Also to Mrs. Roup and
her delightful fourth graders at
Summit View Elementary School
and Mrs. DiPasquale's fifth graders
at Cougar Run Elementary School
who made this a better book
along the way.

Once there was this little boy,
in my primary school,

Some thought he was a joke;
some thought he was real cool.

He sat alone in home room class,
was more than slightly weird;

He wore a dotted, red beret,
and had a wispy beard.

While most kids played at recess
and tossed around a ball,

Joe sprayed his concoctions
on the floors and on the wall.

He shouted up and down the hall,
bacteria! germs! and lice!

He warned the lunch room ladies
of what appeared to be a spice.

He said it wasn't spice at all,
but molds and growing stuff.

Joe could clear the lunch room out,
when we'd all had enough!

When called up to the office,
with Y, his favorite girl

Principal Elmo growled real loud
and stroked his single curl.

"But you don't understand!" said Joe;
"This place is quite a mess!

If we don't warn the students now,
their stomachs will distress!"

Then Joe leaned over Elmo's desk,
he whispered in his ear,

He motioned to his derby'd head
"So soon it will appear!"

He told him that the potion had
put whiskers on his chin.

So, maybe too on Elmo's head?
They both began to grin.

The potion grew a little beard,
on Joe's face way too young,
and when he licked his fingers off,
it grew right on his tongue.

He told Elmo of his plan.
While his grandpa took a nap,

he'd sprinkled his new potion,
right under grandpa's cap.

Joe talked about how he was proud,
of grandpa's new hairdo.

"A patch of thick hair sprouted,
where once were just a few!"

Then Elmo sent Joe on his way
and pondered if he should.

He sprayed the stuff atop his head;
"It really might look good!"

What Joe did then at science fair,
really set him off apart.

It's where the legend of Fountain Joe,
really got its start.

There in his little bottle,
he claimed to hold the key,

"To rid the earth of all disease,
You all just wait and see!"

"Don't drink from
that there fountain!"
He'd shout up on a stool,

"Please let me clean it off first,
where germs can really pool!

There lurking on that handle,
is little J.J.'s cold,

Ethan has the Hong Kong flu,
don't say that you weren't told!

And swirling in that water,
in the bottom of that trough,

is influenza, pink eye,
and I'm sure the
whooping cough."

The next day here at my own school,
Joe couldn't get a rest.

His show had made them all afraid,
they put Joe to the test.

So everyone here at my school,
shelled a quarter out to Joe.

Lines formed around the fountain
and wherever he would go.

They'd pause to enter doorways;
and wait to flush the john,

'Til Joe sprayed off the handle,
with patience they would yawn.

Joe discussed with his friend Y
what she thought he should do,

to make his potion ready
for more than just the few.

He wondered how it might work,
to produce his stuff in mass.

He needed a good manager,
he thought Y was the lass.

Then Y got a great idea,
"Why one quarter at a time?

If we could make a package,
Joe's fame would surely climb!"

Y started thinking big,
"We could really make some cash!

For if the potion grew some hair,
it would surely be a smash!"

"When they
see what
they are
touching,
they'll wish
they had my mix

"For just three dollars and some change, their health you can affix."

So, Joe and Y
worked day and night,
he mixed and she assembled.
They were a perfect little team,
a romance they resembled.

Yes, people
all would hear some day
how Joe had found a cure.

"Up there with Doctor Salk one day!"
Of this he was quite sure.

And on that day Joe
magnified his nasty petri dish;
when we all looked into that glass,
Joe got his special wish.

Every student in our school,
bought a kit from little Joe,
From the fortune he had made,
much further he would go.

They appeared
at school with boxes full,
piled high up to the ceiling.

When Principal Elmo stumbled in,
he really started reeling.

But when he heard and
saw the stuff that Joe
was showing there,

He pulled some bills
from his own wallet,
the first in line to care.

Joe and Y went to Elmo's house,
and asked to see his crown.

Then Elmo smiled his widest smile;
no longer had a frown.

For resting on some antlers there,
were derby hats galore.

And on his head were his own curls,
from the back up to the fore.

They whistled and they skipped around,
Joe stroked his bearded cheek.

He'd done it right, he knew
for sure, a potion with a tweak!

His potion cleaned away the germs,
and grew a little hair.

Seems he had found the secret,
now folks would really care!

And last I heard; young Joe
is rich and married to Yvonne,

A microbiologist billionaire
from that potion he did spawn.

So that's how Drinking Fountain Joe,
who seemed a little weird,

left Bennett Elementary School,
with his beret and wispy beard.

Drinking Fountain
Joe's Glossary

Drinking Fountain Joe
the main character of this story.

Glossary a list of terms in a special subject, field or area of usage, with accompanying definitions. These terms are not in alphabetical order, but in the order that they appear in the book. We hope the following glossary will help you to enjoy the story of Drinking Fountain Joe better.

primary of, pertaining to, or characteristic of primary school; *the primary grades.*

wispy any small or thin tuft, a wisp of hair. *Seen in the classic comb over. Ear to ear wisps.*

concoctions A substance made by combining ingredients; *root beer and vanilla ice cream.*

undies Informal. Underwear. Not really in book, just a fun word to say. *Boxers or briefs?*

bacteria any of numerous microscopic organisms contributing to the production of disease.

germs a micro-organism, when disease-producing; microbe. *ie: boy germs to girls, vice versa*

lice pl. of louse. Parasitic insect on man and other mammals. *Lice are not nice!*

distress that which causes pain, suffering, danger, etc. *An older sibling causes great distress at times.*

potion a drink or draft, esp. one having or reputed to have medicinal or magical powers.

whiskers single hairs of the beard when combined make a face "whiskered". *Rough stuff.*

pondered to consider something deeply or thoroughly. *Such as why I am reading these terms?*

lurking to lie or wait in concealment, skulk, sneak, prowl.

trough a long, narrow, open receptacle, usually box like in shape. *Joe's cough trough.*

influenza an extremely contagious, commonly epidemic disease. *Flu = poo 4 you.*

whooping cough an infectious disease of the respiratory mucous membrane, esp. of children.

john Informal for toilet. *Though if your name is John, you'd rather it wasn't.*

assembled to put or fit together, at an assembly the kids are put together, *(wow they're loud).*

resembled to be like or similar to. *My sister most resembled a movie star named Lassie.*

Salk Dr. Jonas Edward, born 1914, U.S. bacteriologist: developed Salk vaccine. *Very Cool Dude.*

petri-dish a shallow, circular dish used for culturing bacteria and other micro-organisms.

reeling to sway or rock under a blow, shock etc. *With all these terms my mind is reeling!*

crown the top of the head, *remember "Jack fell down and broke his crown."*

fore abbreviation for front, forehead, fore-front. *Oh fore the love of Pete (no "e" really).*

microbiologist a scientist dealing with the structure, function, use of microscopic organisms.

spawn to produce, to give rise to. *The salmon spawned a new business in his salmon egg shop.*

Synchrocyclotron Physics term. A type of cyclotron that synchronizes its accelerating voltage with particle velocity in order to compensate for the relativistic mass increase of the particle as it approaches the speed of light. *This has nothing to do with this book, but if you understood it, what are you doing in elementary school?*